KU-394-355

The Monster Party

A humorous
rhyming story

First published in 2005 by
Franklin Watts
96 Leonard Street
London
EC2A 4XD

Franklin Watts Australia
45–51 Huntley Street
Alexandria
NSW 2015

A CIP catalogue record for this book is available
from the British Library.

ISBN 0 7496 6127 5 (hbk)
ISBN 0 7496 6133 X (pbk)

Series Editor: Jackie Hamley
Series Advisors: Dr Barrie Wade, Dr Hilary Minns
Design: Peter Scoulding

Printed in Hong Kong / China

The Monster Party

Written by
Damian Harvey

Illustrated by
Jane Cope

W
FRANKLIN WATTS
LONDON•SYDNEY

Damian Harvey

"Monsters always seem miserable so I thought I'd cheer them up with a party – but not everyone likes noisy parties!"

Jane Cope

"I really had fun making the pictures for this book. Mice are great to draw. But I'm not sure why this mouse is blue!"

High on the hill is a
haunted house,

Where nothing stirs –
not even a mouse.

But on the stroke of 12 o'clock,
That haunted house begins to
ROCK!

7

The ghosts and ghouls
begin to moan.

A coffin lid opens wide

And wakes the one asleep inside.

Uncle Vlad jumps right out,
Claps his hands and gives a shout:

Music starts in the big ballroom.
It's "Elbow Bones and the
Busted Broom".

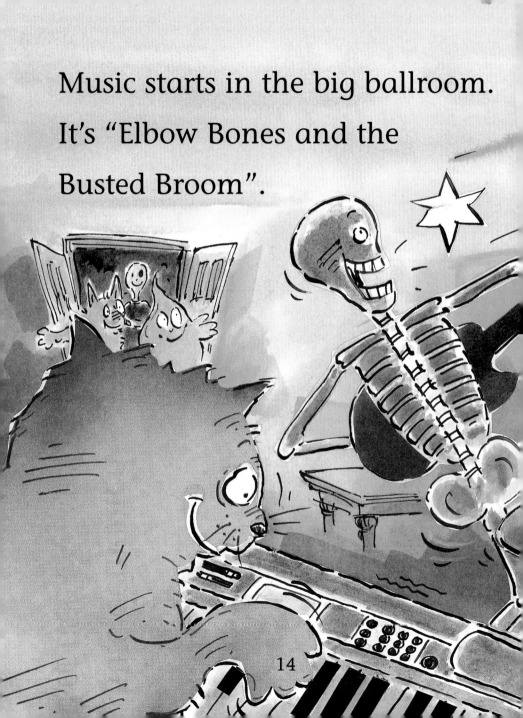

14

At Uncle Vlad's big party bash,

They do the Tango ...

... and the Monster Mash.

17

They bang their heads,

they knock their knees.

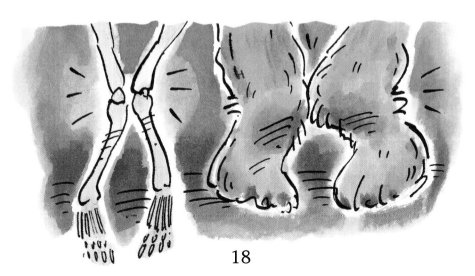

A werewolf scratches at his fleas.

They do the Cancan and stamp
their feet,

Then shake their brains to the
monster beat!

The mummy does a rap:
one, two, three, four.

The crowd goes wild
and howls for more!

The party goes on
all through the night.

And they won't stop until daylight.

But this little mouse has had his fil

Of monster parties up on the hill.

He's sick and tired
of that monster riot,

So he jumps on the table
and shouts:

Now there's peace and quiet
in the haunted house,

And nothing stirs –

not even a mouse!

Notes for parents and teachers

READING CORNER has been structured to provide maximum support for new readers. The stories may be used by adults for sharing with young children. Primarily, however, the stories are designed for newly independent readers, whether they are reading these books in bed at night, or in the reading corner at school or in the library.

Starting to read alone can be a daunting prospect. READING CORNER helps by providing visual support and repeating words and phrases, while making reading enjoyable. These books will develop confidence in the new reader, and encourage a love of reading that will last a lifetime!

If you are reading this book with a child, here are a few tips:

1. Make reading fun! Choose a time to read when you and the child are relaxed and have time to share the story.

2. Encourage children to reread the story, and to retell the story in their own words, using the illustrations to remind them what has happened.

3. Give praise! Remember that small mistakes need not always be corrected.

READING CORNER covers three grades of early reading ability, with three levels at each grade. Each level has a certain number of words per story, indicated by the number of bars on the spine of the book, to allow you to choose the right book for a young reader:

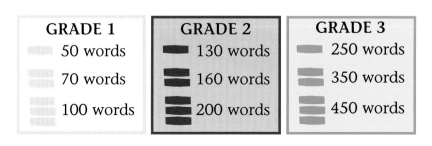

GRADE 1	GRADE 2	GRADE 3
50 words	130 words	250 words
70 words	160 words	350 words
100 words	200 words	450 words